# INTO THE DARK

SOMBRATA MUKHERJEE

"To my friend, Sumandrila Das - an early writing companion

My Motherly Bengali teacher - Mitra Chowdhury,
And as always my Sir, Biswajit Das – my foundation of English"

# Contents

# Preface

Unnatural events are after us, as much as we are after them. Want to experience a few? Well, prepare yourself to walk past some of the weirdest of incidents witnessed by the author himself. A travel to a lone hill, a walk with friends, a stay in an unusual hotel room, a trip on bus, a cat's way and some others.

Based on some real historical events as in the castle of France, to the lost legend in a city of Gujarat, each of them has secrets lying beneath. Not everyone gets a chance to find reality, but in through here – you can get a glimpse. Everyone loves to visit something which beyond this material world, and this book could act as a portal to your wish.

Through this ten spine-chilling suspense and breath-taking facts enter a world beyond the mere scientific explanations. You yourself will be startled to stand on Shakespeare's lines: 'There are many more things in heaven and earth that would never be dreamt in your philosophy'.

Acknowledgements

As always, too many to start with, but the prized amount of inspiration which I received this time to write this collection was from my friends. Wherever and whenever I went with them, something or the other twisted within. I was getting a hung habit to travel with them just for plots.

To name them (which I must) were Arka Basu, Sourav Ray – these two which I must spell at first before anyone else. I constantly used to travel in the afternoons after lunch, and still now whenever they suggest *'Ajke berobi? Ray'o asche'* (Will you go out today? Ray, means Sourav Ray, is also coming), if not in a serious obstruction – I never denied them. Arka, although a Bengali literature lover, often pushes me for my writing and never denies his help wherever possible. Sourav walks with us with his cycle – a precious retrospective element which tunes my most stories. I went to countless places with them, travelling through hidden alleys, abandoned roads, grassy fields and where not. Every trip stockpiled something new to write. We drink tea in the station, on the platform and even ride trains just for the sake of travelling unknowingly. This gives me several plots to work upon.

While travelling with Samadrito Das and Neeladri Shekhar Bhowmik, I conjured some different sort of friendly plots. One of my most favorite elements is Samadrito's mischief and his laughter at his own act. A great deal of narrative power was dragged by me out of it. Songbit Karmakar is another of the book lover (I don't know, it's just he who states so!) who pre-placed the upcoming of my books always. I don't carry any information of how much he reads my books, but the affection he shows for me as writer makes up all. He is one of my old friends who aspires me to be a famous rather than a popular (as he always says!) author.

Another important person which I must mention is Sumandrila Das. Yes, she is a school friend of mine, and my first unofficial writing partner. While in school, we used to work on a set of paranormal series – 'Adventures of John and Alice'. It never got published, but sculpted my writing abilities from an early age. It provided me a platform where I would write in whatever style I would. At a later period, when we received our smart phones – I used to text her relating every story plots of mine. She always wanted that I may publish something as a writer. She always appreciated my works, writing, pointed my flaws, in short – extracted the greater writer within me. Even in regards with this book, she is my first reader as she went through each of my stories in here – providing a very personal review of her own.

And as among the writers, Ruskin Bond played a major role in not just my writing but my whole life. Every time I read his works, I'm transferred to some different world within the laps of Dehra and its mountains. It was to an extent that whenever I was troubled to find a plot, I read his books and somehow or the other – I definitely found something to write on. He is my personal teacher who always aids my writing spirit. Apart from him, my Sir Biswajit Das is another of my prized assets – whom I reckon as my foundation in English.

My publisher is undoubtedly way too friendly than I thought. It is for them only that today I'm a recognized author. I would label Rohan Nath (my publisher) as a friend of mine rather than just a commercial partner who gossips with me over topics which are sometimes beyond the regular works of printing, editing and publishing. I feel way to much free to discuss with him anything I want. He often provides me with suggestions, marketing ideas, themes, story settings, concepts which always made my books better. A lot of thanks to him and his entire team.

Last but not the least, as always, mention should be made of Felu, my cat, who provides me company by napping beside me on the writing desk. When there is no one while I'm writing, he's always there. I cuddle him for a while to massage my fingers (well that's some different context!).

# About The Author

Sombrata Mukherjee is a newborn writer who is now writing professionally over the past few years. He has had a passion for writing from a very young age, literally even before finding the essence in reading. He used to listen to the Legendary tales of Indian History, Gods from his late grandmother Gouri Mukherjee. This stirred him to write something equally mesmerizing. This grew up a passion for writing within him, even before he started to read by himself at a later period. He started his unofficial writing journey from an early age of around ten with comic strips, poems and stories. Scarcely had they carried meanings but the talent to compose in future was foreshadowed.

At the age of 19, Sombrata published his first book *'Temptations'*, a collection of classical love poetry (completed while he was 17). Next, he published the book *"What every Hindus need to know about Hinduism"* (a complete work on Hindu, part 1). Earlier, he wrote a variety of unpublished short stories, including *'My Last Day in Park Street Cemetery'*, *'Along With Us, Disloyal'*, and such. This book has the complete work of ten unpublished stories in a collection till yet.

Mukherjee also has a great passion for his native Bengali and has composed works in the language *like 'Bipin Babur Camera', 'Nikhilda Samagra', 'Haariya Pheliyachi', 'Bigyaner alap sahitter songe'*, and others. He has worked in over three English anthologies magazines, and was nominated in INBW (India's Next Big Writer) and has its certificate. Sombrata is also the possessor of the prestigious 21st Emily Dickinson Award (for his book 'Temptations') and the Jane Austen Award from Book Leaf Publishing.

Sombrata passed out from St. Judes High school Madhyamgram with Computer Science and is currently pursuing the stream of Mass Communication and Journalism at Amity University Kolkata. He often tells of getting a combined inspiration from his parents, chiefly from his mother, Soma, who inspired him to read and write to a greater extent. Mukherjee's father, Subrata, is the possessor of various children's comics (chiefly in Bengali), magazines which mesmerized Sombrata's taste in comics and Literature. The young writer has a great interest in classic genres starting from novels to short stories, poems and plays and is often inspired by classic writers.

'You can hear Literature', says he, 'even when it does not speaks, and that's the essence. It is beyond praise and possesses the ability to stir your mind, even though you are reading a book sitting in a particular corner.'

# Introduction

Who is the one who completely dislikes macabre tales? Even some of the renounced writers of the world were great tellers of suspense like Sir Arthur Conan Doyle, Anton Chekhov, William Sydney Porter (O. Henry), our very own Rabindranath Tagore and others. Even India's one of the most favorite story teller Ruskin Bond have a stock pile of countless spine-chilling tales.

It was after a long time I decided to work on some macabre collection which I thought would excite most readers. After publishing two of my recent books, my readers suggested me to go on to some mysterious tales. Initially I thought of something big to work with but preferred short stories later because most readers like suspense in short pages. This was the dawn of another problem as writing short stories is not a child's play and requires a lot more dedication than even a novel composure. I read various texts from various authors and started to scribble anomalously sitting on my writing desk.

I was still standing blank until one day a plan to visit Park Street with my school friend Sumandrila initiated my spirit. I wrote my first story 'My last day in Park Street' literally even before I went there. It was out of my mere imagination which settled down on paper through my pen. It was followed by Disloyal, Along with us, and the list of the index goes on. 'My last day in Park Street' and 'Disloyal' has already been published in two anthologies on which I worked as a co-author. But today all the tales of macabre has been packed up in this single book 'Into the Dark'.

This title was selected as most stories in here are set when the sun sets. There is a well known Bengali proverb which states: *'Jekhane bagher bhoy, seikhanei sondheye hoy'* (Where there's a fear of tiger, there it must be dusk). When there is an absence of light, certain things emerges out to set an impression over the minds of people. Most conceive it supernatural; others try to grasp it through scientific postulates. Writers on the other hand pen the incidents down for a better understanding and also for a source of entertainment to the readers. No dought most writers who wrote so many macabre tales must have somehow or the other underwent through some weird experiences. These they shaped down in the form of writing through the power of their pen.

This was one of my first tries in composing a collection of short stories mostly inspired from my real life incidents. This book also has a few stories relating to historical events, chiefly inserted to break the pattern flow and again suit-up for the upcoming tales. Hopefully you will like it and please whenever possible let me know if any suggestion for this book or ideas regarding an upcoming book is there within you. Every comment will be gladly accepted.

You may contact me through my email:- sombratamukherjee@gmail.com

***" Imagination Is***
***Something Which***
***The Reality Longs "***

***" Sombrata Mukherjee "***

# I

# My last day in Park Street

I was like always in a hurry so I never got a chance to look properly towards the Calcutta park street cemetery, although I passed by the spot almost regularly. I worked as a manager in one of the park street restaurants, but one day something happened which forced me to leave my job.

Monday was usually a busy day for many, but for me – it was an off. The park street was a great area for me to roam about then. It is famous itself for the countless number of restaurant and pubs, but my job place was already in a restaurant so I wasn't interested by them. The famous park street cemetery was something which used to excite me. A very old caretaker used to guard the place throughout the day, assisted by a little girl – hardly ten as felt. I didn't know the relation between the two but they seemed to be much used to with each other.

One day I held two cups of tea, one for the old caretaker and one for me so we could have some gossip. The girl roamed around the age old graves but quite silently, very often fixing her frowning sight on a rather small broken grave. She often seemed like was highly depressed of something.

I surely talked with the old man, but never asked about the girl. I felt sometimes that why her grandfather (I assumed the old man to be) allowed her to walk alongside the graves – but to my surprise she didn't displayed the slightest bit of fright in her. She roamed freely here and there even when the day turned dim.

One day around nine when I was returning from my job at night, I saw the old caretaker's chair outside the cemetery but occupied by that gloomy girl. For the first time ever, I got a chance to talk with her. Something was unusual about her; she always seemed to be upset of something. I was the first one, who broke over the ice.

- "What's your name girl?"

- "Maya"

- "Where's uncle?"

- "He went to the nearby shop to bring in a cup of tea, he drinks often to keep himself awake"

- "Why are you out alone in this night?"

- "I feel better"

The ending words parted from her lips in a cold note. Who on earth feels better roaming around a graveyard? I knew that the park street cemetery was famous but not so much that a little girl, barely ten, would roam around it all day. While I was thinking all these I noticed that the girl kept looking at the small broken grave – the same one which she was staring at in the morning.

"Did someone close to you died?" I asked out of sympathy.

"No", she said with a sad note.

"Then why you always seem so upset?" my curiosity gained height.

Something unusual happened at the moment – something which made me lose my senses; the girl pointed her index finger to the small grave which she was staring at. A cold sobbing voice of the girl unlike the one heard before answered me, "I might have been twenty by now, nobody came to my funeral when I died."

# II

# Disloyal

Edmund was invited to his far living maternal aunt. The term 'far living' is really true. The journey was a long one. He left out early in the morning getting a few days off previously from his publishing office. He loved his job, yet he wasn't completely reluctant to visit his aunt, as he had a close connection with the location. It was the place where he grew, the place where he went to the market holding his aunt's finger, it was the place where he once played with his friends (many of them have lost by now). He had forgotten many a things about that place; a visit might replenish them again.

Early in the morning at around six-thirty, he packed his bag and left for his aunt. Years have passed he last came in contact with his aunt, infact he might pose some difficulty finding the house. The journey though a long one, was really adventurous in the lap of mountains. On a bus travel, he only stopped to drink some tea both quenching his thirst and energizing him in the cold temperature. When he was halfway to his destination, it was half past noon. The mail service (as he knew) up in this hill was slow as compared with the plains, so he decided he would hit up in her house straightway.

Edmund was feeling hungry by now, the journey was somewhat feeling unending. It was about three, and he hasn't eaten anything except two cups of tea. When the bus stopped, it was four thirty. Finally he was there. He noticed that the place had somehow changed. There were new shops in possessions, small commercial buildings, a new postal network (he didn't knew about the new post service or else he might have sent a letter). The general area though hasn't changed a bit. The same cobbled roads, the same protruded house balconies, and the same hug of nature.

As predicted, he was facing trouble searching his aunt's home. Where was she? He couldn't blame the situation as it has been almost past 35 years he last came here, or maybe even more.

When the sun was almost hiding behind the hills, a stranger out of nowhere walked towards him,

"Out here somewhere?" asked the stranger.

"Yes, I'm here to find my aunt's house. She I suppose lives in the privet square." Spoke out Edmund blankly in a hope if someone could guide him.

"Privet square is at least six miles more from here," said the stranger directly.

Now what? Thought Edmund. It was nearly five-past thirty and if he had to travel six miles more there would be a night-fall and he would be very late. A lodge nearby could do this night he thought. But to his surprise the only occupied lodge was found near the bus-stand. The place was deserting gradually as the night was darkening. To both his surprise and delight the stranger said him something,

"My home is just up the thirty-two lane, Pringlett square, want to spend the night?"

"Thanks for saying so, but how could I.." stumbled Edmund, "I mean, I don't even know you properly.."

"Don't worry about it," said the stranger casually, "I know you."

Edmund didn't know what to answer. The strangely though felt oddly familiar but wasn't completely clear to Edmund. All he did was followed the old man up the thirty-two lane, Pringlett Square. Within fifteen minutes of time killing, both of them reached a shabby looking place. Edmund was finding a strange familiarity with it – however was once again was unable to express clearly.

"Come in", said the old man with a warm greeting.

Edmund without looking at the old man was much busy scanning the shabby house. It was completely different from exterior; no one could guess that this battered looking exterior shelter had a warm fire place inside, a moderate size kitchen-hall and a warm cozy bedroom welcomed by a hand woven doormat. The place felt connected deep down to Edmund.

The corridor walls were decorated with family pictures. A young sturdy man with a snow-coat and an army cap was visible in one of the picture, which, Edmund reckoned as the old man in his livid ages. It was followed by a little boy's portrait showing his multi-color clothed back holding a small rock in his left hand. Edmund felt the boy strangely familiar, he felt as if he was someone very close to him.

There were few more portraits of an American Husky, a bowl of fruits, an office group photo, and....

"That's!..."

"That's Lily", drowning the shout of Edmund the old man spoke out, "your maternal aunt in her fruitful ages."

Both of them were staring at the portrait of a young, tender woman possessing long and bright sunny locks, wearing a cherry colored red skirt, and holding a flower basket in her left arm.

"What's my aunt's photo doing over here?" asked Edmund out of high curiosity.

"I'll explain," said the old man, "come have a cup of tea"

Edmund was in no mood of having tea right now, but to know about his aunt he was obliged to. The old man went inside the kitchen-hall, spoke with someone and came back. Edmund and he sat in two oppositely facing armchairs inside the fire-lit bedroom.

"Now about Lily," started the old man without properly looking at Edmund, "When was the last time you met with your aunt?"

"From seven years onwards I remember myself with my aunt. She was the one who grew me up until in fifteen I left for the town to study", answered Edmund feeling a bit eerie by the moment.

The fireplace was casting strange shadows on the closed door of the bedroom. Even in the heat, Edmund was feeling the cold running down his spine.

"I see", answered the old man in a grave flat tone, "have you met your aunt after you left for the town? Have you ever returned?"

"I..I..", stammered Edmund, "I never got a chance afterwards, but why are you asking me all these?"

"Do you remember how lively you were Edmund when you stayed with your aunt? Do you remember yourself?" asked the old man.

"I do," answered Edmund getting his voice back, "Atleast I do remember myself. But may I ask you that why this house so familiar is?"

The old man stood up from his armchair now looking distinctively furious, "How could you even speak of the word 'Familiar'

Edmund?", he went on, "You never bothered to look towards your aunt, all you did was completed education, got a job and settled with your family in the plains. You don't even remember your place – it's Pringlett Square, and not Privet Square, how DISLOYAL you were regarding your motherly aunt."

Edmund was already suspicious of how the old man came to know his name, and now all these facts had started to shake him more than ever. He felt guilty now of why he hasn't contacted his aunt in last 35 years. Atleast a moment of his life was worth sacrificing for the lady who took his parent's place and grew him up. Paper weighting his sadness, he asked to the old man,

"Where's she now?"

"Too slow Edmund, after long years when I returned, this place had nothing but only you" said the old man once again in his grave flat tone, "I too left her once. You were just three then, so wouldn't remember me. We had no child, yet I didn't like your presence, but your aunt did. A small trifle was enough for me to leave this place to your aunt and you. She worked hard to grow you; Lily even abandoned me for you. But after you left, the only thing left in here was your memory. The young seven years old child, who loved his aunt more than anything in the world."

The old man sighed and continued, "This is your aunt's place, and the only remnant here is the old you, somehow after you left, your aunt managed to spent time with you before she actually passed away, you must see for yourself."

A feeling of both sadness, and haunt was gripping Edmund by the moment. He was starting to realize how disloyal he truly was. It was kind of impractical to say that within a span of 35 years he never got a chance to meet his loving aunt. The old man was true, he mustn't use the word 'familiar' again, cause' his aunt is no more in this world.

"But then,.." thought Edmund, "who sent him the letter?"

Another thing was starting to stir up in Edmund's mind, what did the old man meant by his aunt's spending time with him after he left Pringlett Square? But to this question, he was answered soon.

There was a sudden knock at the bedroom door. Edmund felt distinctly uneasy as the old man walked towards the door. A tray of two tea and some biscuits were visible in the hands of a young boy. It was the same figure with the same multi-colored clothes he had seen in the portrait, although he now saw the front of it.

This time Edmund had no trouble recognizing the face. It was the seven years old him who used to spend time with his loved aunt once. Edmund was looking at himself only for a very short moment of time before his vision faded out.

# III

# An unusual bus ride

It was a general holiday from work, however work itself never left me. To be honest, if a work is what you love, it won't feel like work anymore. I always tried the best to utilize my leisure in some knowledge absorbing businesses (it didn't work every time though!), and this time it was a tour to Calcutta's international book fair. I've been to book fairs earlier, but this was my second time in Calcutta's one. The last time I was too young to extract the real nectar from there.

As a writer, the act of reading is supplementary to me. When you're feeling filled – write, and when you're feeling empty – read. That's a real principle. In a book fair, even though I really didn't bought too many of the books, but kept a habit of rummaging through them.

I started off from the local bus stand. It was littered with people like moths flying around a source of light. This situation was partly created due to the book fair and partly

(I suppose) of today being Sunday. The waiting wasn't long as there were a horde of buses which kept snatching a handful of passengers. After about ten minutes of sweeping the street dust with my left foot, I found a bus of my convenience. Along with some other, I rushed to capture a window seat – third last in the bus. Many other boarded the bus but they kept clinging for a while till half of the bus was emptied after two-three stops. I was on the benefit as I never had a great appreciation for crowded buses, as it was both difficult to move within and survive in a smelly atmosphere.

After the fifth stop, the bus had an apparent finite number of people, about five to six, including the conductor and the driver. I had to wait for seven more stops before leaving the transport.

The bus felt lonely. The sunny atmosphere kept the weather warm but sometimes irritating when there was a busy crowd outside. My pair seat was empty, but a gloomy looking middle aged man sat on the window seat just on my opposite row. He was busy snuffing his nose in a big newspaper which completely hid his head leaving only his top hat exposed to some extent. An old lady was sitting in a seat behind him, but she too left in the next stop. I looked through the window beside me, the transportation had reduced in this space and a number of moving trees were observed. A few new stalls had also been installed which I have not seen earlier (I was in Calcutta after about a year). The bus halted in a traffic jam after about five minutes of further journey and in this, hopped in a grumpy man followed by a delicate feminine figure. At first, I thought there were father-daughter, but was mistaken when the man dropped off in the next traffic jam without a word and the girl sat next to my seat. I found it interesting as the whole bus had only the conductor, driver, me and that mysterious paper-man. She would have sat anywhere throughout the bus if not right beside me! I didn't mind her presence though, as still being a bachelor – sitting beside a graceful young lady was worth a scene.

She was heavily scenting with the essence of Lavender and Tulsi (an unusual combination, I know, but that was what I felt at that time!) I didn't dare to look into her face (it was difficult to stray my eyes as it often met that paper man sitting adjacently opposite to my seat!), but kept trying. After a few attempts, I deciphered her to be younger than me. She had a moonlit fair complexion, and a brown shaded curly hair. She was wearing a white cotton top paired up with a brownish long skirt to match her mud washed locks. A hand woven side-bad was her companion which had a beautiful fabricated portrait of the world poet R.N Tagore. When the bus speeded, a gust of air came from the paper-man's window and pushed her hair to caress over my face. She as if feeling guilty of the act which she in reality had no control over, started to arrange her hair in her delicate palms.

I wouldn't withstand further. Her dreamy eyes compelled attention and thus even being an introvert, I broke over the ice,

"You're going to the book fair?"

"I was suppose to visit there yesterday", her heart throbbing voice spoke out, "but there was some problem on the way and I failed to reach there on time"

I was very much contended by her way of speaking and somehow felt that she was enjoying my presence. My only distraction was that paper-man who kept on peeping over the paper at me in a face which carried visible signs of disgust.

"Are you going to the fair?", she asked in a clear tone of sweetness.

"Yes, I love reading, writing is also my passion although..."

"So you're a writer too?", she smiled while she said so. I found it difficult to grip whether the statement had a tone of appreciation or mockery, as I was busy swimming in her beauty.

"Don't you have any one with you?", she broke through my thoughts.

"None, actually I'm still a bachelor you know.."

The girl smiled again with mirth and continued, "I mean any relatives or alike accompanying you in the trip?"

I felt drowned in my seat due to the stupidity I made within the conversation. I was too much intoxicated in a complete stranger. Too my good fortune, she apparently enjoyed my stupidity rather than be aggrieved. When the bus slowed at a traffic jam, she arranged her side bag, ready to leave the transport. She left her seat and paved her hand to shake with mine,

"I'm Binya, nice to meet you. Hope to see some other day", and she hopped off from the standing bus. (Although I noticed she didn't pay the fare, or perhaps had given earlier while boarding? I might have missed).

I was as if electrified. How soft and cool was her feminine hand, how tender it felt! I kept on dreaming of her, although I had no idea how I would contact her later. She was even unaware of my name and whereabouts?! Just I knowing her name wouldn't suffice enough to prolong a second meeting. The old man throughout the whole situation kept stupidly staring at me, as if I was a mad man. I didn't bother his reactions as I was lost in thoughts of Binya.

The man kept reading the newspaper for about ten minutes further till he would no longer tolerate the standing bus,

"Isn't the square lane mess settled yet?", he cried from his seat.

"Think so", replied the conductor who just boarded the bus with a cup of tea in his hand, "The event is still making a scene in the busy street, often jamming up the traffic".

The man, now visibly aggrieved, slashed the newspaper in his seat and went towards the conductor. "Keep the change", and he also hopped down from the standing bus, leaving me lonely again. The bus was standing for about twenty five minutes, and I was also feeling really naustic in the sun. I was now the only passenger in the whole bus observing the two service men gossiping with each other onboard. The bus felt eerie, even though it was wide afternoon. I have never in my life witnessed such an empty bus before. Feeling uneasy after five more minutes, I asked the conductor of the traffic jam.

"A local resident on scooter met a car accident yesterday night. The police keep blocking the area for rigorous traffic checks and maintenance of vehicles. This is creating a non-ending jam!"

I tried to look through the open window of my seat, and witnessed a number of patrols in the clearing. Surely there must have been something unusual. Suddenly, I was reminded of the paper-man, and the paper which he was reading. It might carry the piece of information which I was looking for, who knows?

I grabbed the paper from the back seat and leafed through the headline:

"A teenager was struck by a speeding vehicle at the square lane yesterday. Police suspects the victim to be a local resident who was up for the Calcutta book fair and met a terrible fate on the way."

There was a portrait photo of the victim attached below. This simple picture in good condition was too terrible for me to gaze at. I was feeling sick at the moment, as this was the face which I would never ever forget in my life. The caption inscribed below the photo read the victim's name – Binya.

# IV

# Along with Us

That night was mysterious. I always thought why nights were often associated with loneliness, but after that day I know why.

The visit was of the evening, I with my friend went off to visit another friend's home. Two of us were on foot, whereas the other one to whose place we were about to visit was on his cycle. He was leading us the way. The place had some few cottage kind of house, as the area was mostly occupied with vast fields. It was raining slightly before we left for the trip, so the sky was still cloudy – obstructing the slightest of sunlight in the evening. Darkness was engulfing the area slowly.

The streets were partially constructed with cement, blended with earth on top of which weird kind of fungus and plants had started to grow. Few houses as I observed didn't looked like it had anyone inside, although the faint sound of human cough was coming behind from one of the battered doors. The fields were filled with countless puddles which filled the air with the smell of rotten rats. Although few distant human voices could be heard, yet we failed to find a single person on our route.

I never came to such a place before. The region was arousing a feeling of sadness, I felt too much lonely and remorse although I had two more friends by my side. Rumors were the area was once a dump yard to countless dead, murdered by the robbers who raided the place decades ago. An oil mixed stale smell was whimpering along with us. After few minutes of walking we observed a dark skinned cat looking at three of us from a distant wall.

A cup of tea at my friend's home was the only thing which kept us there. The place was unimaginably empty, too much deserted for one to visit. People say they love to travel in solitary places, but this one was deathly. Even street dogs, the slightest hope of noise, were absent. We hastened to finish up the tea to leave at the earliest.

We left our friend's home to continue our journey from three to two people. The return trip was even lonelier. The only companion now was the two shadows of us, scarcely visible under the dim moonlight. There were no street lamps throughout the travel. The rustling of trees broke the silence to some extent but made the atmosphere even more eerie.

A distant howl was mingling in my ear, although I clearly remember that we met no dog on the way. I asked my friend to find the way out in the dark as we were like losing the pace to return. The journey felt like forever, as we longed to leave the area.

After a scope less walk of not less than twenty minutes in the dark, we finally saw a faint ray of light from the main road, entering the inner dark alley on which we were walking. Although the main road was visible, to reach there we had to select one out of two more alleys in front.

Unexpectedly, we saw our friend to whose place we went, resting on his cycle on the turning edge of one alley close to main road. The faint light was coming from there, as he was standing under the only street lamp we deciphered till yet. We weren't surprised though as he knew much more twists and turns than we did on there. He might have took the cycle and sped past us through some shortcuts.

"Sourav", I asked being a bit furious by the moment, "you might have leaded us the way, which lane shall we take now to reach the main road?"

"Tried to see whether you would make it out or not!" he said, giggling a bit. After that he pointed a finger towards an alley, the one on whose wall he was leaning with his cycle.

After the turning, the road was clearly visible with a vibrant burst of light. The alley from which we took the turn was still unavoidably dark, the only light coming from Sourav's pole. I turned back to bid him goodbye.

A strange thing happened at that moment. I don't know whether my friend noticed it or not but there was something uneasy about what I saw. The place where Sourav was leaning over the wall had the light-post attached. It was casting light over Sourav and his cycle to create their shadow on the lonely alley.

Although Sourav was standing there right in front of me, but to my horror, the only shadow visible under the light was of his cycle.

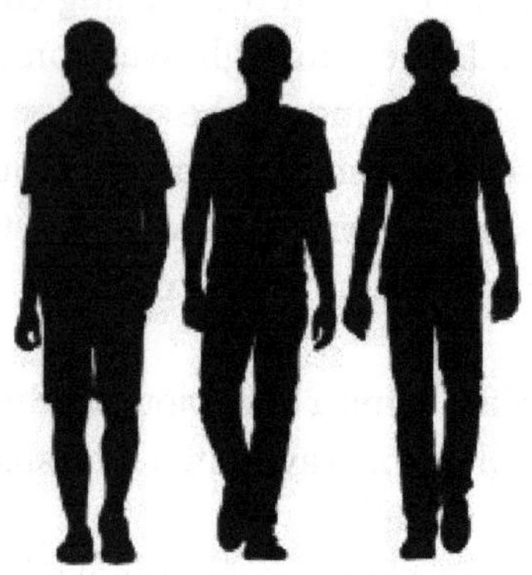

# V

# The Photograph

The foothill of Shillong becomes more beautiful in the warm adoring heat of summer, instead of the winters which most people living in the planes think of. I've been to plains, stayed there while studying and found a job here in the hills. What a luck! Plains usually offer a reduced salary to younger men like us thinking us not as skilled and adaptive like the plain-men. There were onto some stereotypical notion that we hilly people are like some monkeys who hop down from the trees to grab some work opportunity and then again settle back on the tree.

It was nothing like that, I worked here in a hotel serving food to the plain-people proving that sometimes even plane-landers also visit these monkeys. But yes, as per the procedures and customs of living here, holidays appointed to the staff were way too low compared to the plains, and after about a year I got a chance to visit my grandmother. She lived in the hilly terrains of Dhankheti, a less attractive tourist spot and a greater area for natives like us. The Catholic Pastoral Church grounds were near to her residence – magnifying the beauty of that terrain. I used to pay visit to the church as a child holding the hands of my grandma.

There was a two-way bus journey to the place, I packed myself and went off to visit her. It was past ten years when Grandfather had passed, Grandma lived on his pension, always assisted by her maid (which she changed often), and surrounded by trees – which I remember planting as a child with Grandfather.

As I reached to spend the two-weeks holiday with my Grandmother I met her on a string bed kept outside. She was busy with her usual knitting job and overseen my presence for a while I was standing right in front of her.

'Why are you standing like that my dear boy, ask Kamali to prepare you some tea', I was amazed that she did observe my presence, I myself being unaware of the fact.

'Wasn't it Shamali the last year grandma?'

'Yes, I switched her with Kamali. Shamali was too busy munching pan (beetle leaves dressed with various Indian spices, addictives) and coloring her mouth with its juices. You know I'm not used to such and thus I got rid of her'

I sat beside her on the string bed, the touch with it flourished my memories of childhood. Various incidents started to hit the mind as if they were longing for the moment when I would visit in here. I often used to disturb the knitting of Grandma, and although she rebuked me in times but held that authority to herself only. She always defended me from anyone else' rebuke, including my parents and grandfather as she thought that sole authority of scolding me was only limited to her.

Kamali came with two cups of warm tea. Shillong's tea is way light and fragrance filled, unlike the ones found in plains. Some says Assamese tea tastes the best, while some says Darjeeling's tea scent has no match – but to my conclusion, Shillong's tea had the taste of Assam and the scent of Darjeeling. Relishing on the solitary place sitting with Grandma, served tea by Kamali, cherishing the memories – what else a living soul would want?

We continued to converse for a few hours about my current status of living, how well was I doing, what were my plans in the upcoming weary days, and also about Grandma and her days in new Dhankheti. Yes, days were undoubtedly tough for her after the death of my Grandfather – but she was more of a practical lady and was devoid of the slightest spark of imaginative, socio-emotional things. However, that didn't prevent her from discussing my childhood days with me. Kamali was kept in charge of the flower garden which Grandma was very fond of. This was a fact which I hope Kamali knew because any treachery done to a single flower would make her lose the job. I later learnt from Grandma that she was making a scarf for the child of Kamali who was living with her in a nearby village.

In the evening, I entered the cottage resisting the tempting atmosphere outside which would glue anyone. The insides weren't changed a bit excepting the new plaster and a bunch of new floor pots hung within. The kitchen space, double bedded room, and the little space of dining, everything was kept as it is.

The day got spent well. It was not before late at night I found a trunk under my bed. Actually, the bed hooked up a bit from the middle which made me look curious to look under it. I clamped myself down to find a metal trunk. Light was too scare here to look for now, and the only candle was being taken by Kamali who was dressing up for the night. I thought it better to wait for tomorrow before exploring the chest.

The sun dawned early, or, as it seems like in the hills. You could literally experience a horizon (the plane which connects the sky with land) in these plains. Grandma was up before me as I experienced now to be around past five in the morning. Kamali was already engrossed in the chores – sweeping the floor, washing the utensils from last day, and after seeing me, prepared a cup of tea. I took it outside to find Grandma their setting up her knitting accessories. I reckoned that her morning started way earlier than mine and now it was an interval from some work. I didn't forget the trunk from the last night, and it was only after breakfast I sped past Kamali's wiping the floor and dived on the bed. The tin marked its presence by hitting me bluntly in my belly. I took the lid out and opened it to find a treasure stocked within.

Yes, treasure, it was treasure for me. Grandma had this archive since I was little playing in her laps. I found my old trump cards which I once played with my grandfather, a pair of stripped badminton net which lost its partner shuttle cock, a deflated football, some old documents which seemed like pension letters of Grandfather, and a photograph.

It wasn't like an ordinary photograph which you see nowadays. It had a distinctive appearance as if carrying a good history with it. The black and white frame was occupied by a young girl possible around six wearing a long skirt, handful of bangles, and possessing a mid-length wavy hair. The smile she had was mischievous, as seemed as if forcefully protruded. She was standing outside in front of a scratched, worn out wall surrounded by various creepers. A few dahlias were also visible in a smudged manner inside the frame. I've seen these kinds of photographs earlier, but I was completely blank about this girl. No time in my life

I remember seeing with this girl nor I've seen this photograph earlier, but to be really honest, I felt a close connection with her. It felt like I know her, but still it felt like I've never seen here. The current situation of me was really unexplainable as I couldn't figure anything. Grandma might have some clues regarding the same, thinking of it I left the room leaving the trunk open to meet grandma outside.

She was not there; instead I met with Kamali who sitting on the string bed – visibly tired of her constant chores.

'Where is grandma?'

'She just now went to the neighbor's, said she won't return till lunch'

Now what? When did she make this routine to gossip with neighbors? However, I didn't mind at this because this much solitude in here would be too much for someone to handle and one really needs someone to gossip and chat with. But I was in an insecure mood. I really wanted to know who this little girl in the photo was and I knew that no one but grandma would answer me. I waited; Grandma came an hour before lunch. I used this opportunity to take the photograph and inquire about it sitting outside on the string bed.

'Yes, I know her very well. Infact, I thought that you would also easily tell who she is'

'Who is she?'

'I can't tell you that. But yes, I can tell you about the photograph'

'But why so? Alright, tell me about the photo atleast'

'You can see this wall behind her? It was our old roof's shed. It was the place where once you played badminton with Ramlal, the son of Basanti – one of our old maids. I guess you forgot her, whatever, this is that place. This photo was clicked by your grandfather. I was busy somewhere else, maybe with you inside the room.'

'But I really cannot recall anything about her, who is she?'

'I told you that I can't answer. If you can figure it out yourself its well enough, or else I won't help in this case.'

'She really seems to be an extrovert'

'Good going, yes she was. You can tell from her looks that she was made to wear such decent dress with force just for this photo which is now the only remmanent of her.'

'Yes,'

'She was a little mischief often fooling around with us. Your Grandfather really appreciated this appearance of her though.'

'I really can't get who she was, I mean, she was so much mixed with you all and there's nothing I do remember of her'

Gradma stood up from her knitting process ready to appear for the lunch. She gave Kamali a shout to set the plates while she continued with me,

'I guess you'll never be able to decipher who she was. She is visible only in this photo, you'll never see or hear of her – this photo is the only piece of her presence as I stated earlier'

'So who is it?'

Grandma smiled while answering, 'Your Grandfather always wanted a daughter to accompany him. His only child left him long ago, and there are you from him. He made you dress like a daughter of his dreams. You were totally against such appearance at that time but Grandfather somehow managed to make you wear these clothes which he brought from a local store. The joy you brought him that day can only be recollected from this photograph which I managed to preserve still today'.

# VI

# Die Musik

After his father's transfer at France in the active years of the Second World War, this was Richard's first time in here. His mother was a music teacher in Berkshire, the Eton where he also once read. Although in France, Richard's only knowledge about this nation was through the French classes he attended in his times.

French was not really a subject of appreciation for Richard but he was always ready to applaud for its historic cultures and standards. He was eager to visit here as during his father's era he was only subjected to studies and was pressed to have a grip over the music lessons taught by his mother – a very personal teacher. In 1945, Richard's father Henry died in a fatal plane crash while serving the British Royal Air force through the French Resistance Forces. By that time, Benito Mussolini, the dictator of Fascist Italy and his mistress Claire were killed by the nationalists themselves and the new emperor of Badoglio surrendered to the Allies. This was a greater victory for the Allied forces and the end of World Wars was also at its dawn.

Richard provided solitude and introvercy an upper hand over all other. Being almost alone from childhood, he was repelled by anyone else's company and thus came to see France all by himself. Due to some benefits of his father in the air force – the minimal problem to land here also diminished.

He spent a few days in France unless one day he got informed about the Castle of the Duke of Savio by a local informant. Castles usually provides a tinge about fairy tales, or old prohibited ruins of princely states but this was ever open to the visitors although the place increasingly witnessed fewer. As a matter of discovery, Richard was interested to pay a visit to Chambery, Savoie chiefly due the attraction of the music room, where still ball dances were said to persist. Music was a part of him now, and thus anything related to it had a tendency to propel him up.

Just similar to different tourist destinations, this place housed a number of guides of which Richard found one. There were not much visitors this time, as he learnt, the crowd count usually was low over there in mid-winters and this was November. This sight compelled appreciation as if it was the only gift which might bring happiness to Richard's visit. The exterior was just like any other ordinary castle, except some protruded rigid ends housing unknown compartments, a narrow died out garden shed and a large rigid doorway allowing the guests to enter the premises. Chateau des Duce de Savoie, the complete name for the shortened 'Duke of Savoy's Castle' was the 11$^{th}$ century structure which principally housed the prefectures, the country council. Historic records witnesses this building to be rebuild several times, last one dating around the First World War. Still throughout these, any artistic eye would be tantalized by the beauty which the stones radiated. The castle had a kiss of royalty blended with the cultural traits of old France. Various princely articles, dusty rooms and erected walls holding memories within would be deciphered. Several locked rooms within it carried a brink of sadness and somehow was seen upon as morose, as if the tied walls had something to say.

Chateau des Duce de Savoie was opened as a tourist spot only after around twenty years post the end of the Second World War of 1945. Adolf Hitler, the dictator of Germany had also committed suicide in an underground bomb shelter by then, marking the defeat of Nazi rule. The defeat of Japan afterwards marked the end of Rome-Berlin-Tokyo Axis, and then the United Nations was also established. Peace sprung around throughout Europe and people were satisfied after the dragged wars. However, there were certain matters which were pressed deep down in the pages of History, never ever to be revealed again. Richard was to witness one of them.

"What a piece of chiseling, can't imagine of its consistency!", said Richard praising a general pillar in front of the guide.

"Several years of hard works, and several years demolished," continued the guide dusting a brick plane by rubbing his index finger over it, "yet few untouched walls carry large secrets. Yes that's the consistency of a generic architect who maximized the possibility to keep the structures similar"

"Was this hall only known for its importance in the Country Council? Wasn't there anything to entertain the guests?", asked Richard.

They walked upstairs and halted before an encased room while the guide continued, "As far work is concerned, the French monarchs never prioritized anything higher;

however 'Die Musik' room was a great attraction for people, until..."

They were interrupted by a young lady who swept past wearing a traditional French hat and long reddish garment. She glanced at their conversation and for a while kept staring the encased room in front of them. For a while she suddenly seemed to be distressed and unhealthy of something as she pressed her forehead and finally moved on.

"What's 'Die Musik'?", asked Richard

"It's a German word for 'The Music'"

"Why a German name in a castle full of French Manor?"

"It seeks some History young man," continued the guide looking at the encased room beside them, "After the seizure of the Alsace-Lorraine in the Franco-Prussian war by the Germans; all that was left of the area was pebbles and stones. Each and every mining court was destroyed and what remained was used to coal up for the Rhine valley military training and areas around it. Alsace-Lorraine was returned back to France only after the German defeat in the First World War of 1914-1918. This match was signed by the League of Nations, of which France was also a part, under a treaty when the then German ruler Kaiser Wilhelm II abandoned his throne and fled to Netherlands!"

Richard was gulping down the Historical records, as this was a subject which he praised above all. Seeing the spark of interest in the portrait of Richard, the guide continued,

"The peace treaties organized by the League of Nations did some major changes in the World History like division of Austria and Hungary to separate nations, reclaiming the lost independences, restoring the Alsace-Lorraine yet still there is this most important 'Treaty of Versailles' – the Paris Peace Conference, attended in 1919 at the Hall of Mirrors.

This treaty ensured the Germans were suppressed to bits and pieces. When the First World War ended, many prisoners of the German War were held captive and were tortured to death."

"And then?"

"Five of them captured were army-musicians who used to entertain the German forces in spare timings. On request, they were granted a wish of how they wanted to die. The penta-musicians wanted a separate room full of musical equipments where they would be locked together and forever till their last breathe. They were granted the wish but during such constant ongoing wars, no such place on that immediate basis was to be found. This Castle of the Duke of Savoy was undergoing constructions due to the damages it received from the First World War, and as per planned a separate room for these penta-musicians were to be allocated under the old-traditional room of Savoie where they lived for two years until passing out. The old music room was renovated over those cemented bodies changing the traditional name of 'La Musica' to 'Die Musik' marking the History of those German musicians"

"What a record!", said an Amazed Richard, "this information totally dumbfounded me as I was never aware of such pieces. Those penta-musicians as you said really loved music didn't they, so as accordingly ended their last breathe with Music!"

"Yes, the French government also approved their honor and thus kept the German name in this whole Castle of French"

Loving the events at play Richard thanked the guide and tipped him for narrating such a beautiful History, even more beautifully. He stepped down the stairway stones and lodged off outside. On his way to the lodge Richard grabbed a copy of 'The Contemporary World' to have a much more knowledgeable grip on these subjects. Night fell, alone seems alright, until you properly experience being alone. The place where he was staying housed him as the only guest around the grassy hilly region, as due to curb unnecessary expenses he avoided costly hotel rooms. This was the room of a French resident, who allowed him to stay for a week.

Dawn came; Richard having the habit of rising early got hold of a newspaper and ran to the room old owner for English translating. He loved keeping record of local news and used the old man as a cheap translator.

The Headline flashed: "Another death recorded from the 'Dis Musik' visit at Chateau des Duce de Savoie. Government suspects unusual activities and plans to suspend tourist visits till further investigations are cleared off"

"This is the $4^{th}$ this year", spoke out the old man in whatever English accent he would deliver. "You were lucky young to have a visit to the Castle of Savoie, especially the 'Die Musik', as the government keeps on closing and opening it for tourist visits"

The newspaper in its usual pattern was read further,

***Miss Amelie the popular ballad mistress was seen leaving the***
***Castle of Savoie in a visibly troubled state. A pedestrian says to witness***
***her suddenly dropping in the street getting unconscious. The locals took her off to***
***the nearest hospital where she was declared dead. Post-mortem***
***reports are yet to be delivered meanwhile police intervention was***
***also being initiated. Government steps up marking the spot as a matter***
***of higher concern as unusual deaths are taking place.***

There was a photo of the lady attached, which Richard immediately recognized as the visitor wearing that traditional French cap with that Reddish outfit.

"This is really unusual," continued Richard, "a general death for visiting a tourist spot recorded in a news story? Might have been any usual way for her death, why the reports are highlighting the Castle of Savoie?"

"The $4^{th}$ death this year, that's it."

"Can you Sir please explain that matter clearly?"

"Every year there are five. Chateau des Duce de Savoie witnessed the fourth death this year. There would the last one to end this cycle

"The last one?"

"Yes, I don't know how many of them keep a record of the prophecy established by those five musicians who used to entertain the German Nationalist forces. There was a change of spices. The musicians pleaded to the court of law that they were only entertainers and not the supporters of Nazi aggressors. They were paid in terms only to entertain the armed lot. The judiciary turned a deaf ear to the suppressed pleas and as a factual request stuffed them up in a closed cemented room under the traditional room of 'La Musica'. This traditional room was later rebuilt post World Wars and named under the current form 'Die Musik'. However the bodies underneath still lay with all the musical equipments and as per sayings those penta-musicians plays the tune of sorrows to attract someone connected with music. The one, who hears so, can't be saved from death. Every year there is a death count of five, the prey of five musicians who visits 'Die Musik' place. The four others died this year after their visit to Chateau des Duce de Savoie. Somehow or the other the deaths are always connected to Music."

Richard's head was spinning rapidly. Is that for the same reason Miss. Amilie pressed her forehead and felt unconscious? Was she trying to block the sound of the lament which was only audible to her? As per the news report, she was a ballad teacher – thus connected to music, and had died. That guide also now somehow felt suppressed about what he was conveying.

The mesmerizing tour came to Richard as a horrific incident unfolded. He felt that some unknown History of the world he came to know of. The book which he bought of the World History scarcely carried incidents as such, and that too is common. Historical texts are often found busy portraying the political spearheads and not of the foundation of countless people who laid them. Nevertheless, he felt a strong urge to return back England and luckily the day after tomorrow's early flight would take him off.

Having a little food at night Richard crawled into his sheets. The bed lamp was still on while he was looking outside in the firefly lit forest. With the light buzzing of cicadas, the environment was no doubt charming and had the ability to make anyone fall asleep at night. Richard was no exception to it as he switched off the bed light and went off to a re-energizing sleep.

Past midnight, he without any reason woke up sitting straight on the bed. The fireflies were still hovering outside like golden orbs circling the grassy bushes. The sound of the cicadas was however replaced with that of a slow distinct lament. This was not any usual lament though. For the first time ever in his life Richard felt horrified for learning and getting connected with music. It enabled him to clearly understand the death lament that was coming from nowhere but the 'Die Musik' room of Chateau des Duce de Savoie.

# VII

# The Professor

I was sixteen then and living in my hometown Kolkata. At that time my mother was doing a beautician course in some other part of the city staying rented near to her institute, while I stayed with my father in our home. It was chiefly due to my school which was a walking distance from my place that I did choose to stay with father.

While staying here, I had a great furry companion – a tabby cat, which I adopted from a young lady a year back then. He used to company me (apart from a cup of tea!) sitting, and mostly napping on my writing desk. As Ruskin Bond says, “For a Writer, even the company of fly is a warm welcome”. I did not mind him as his absence and presence was almost equal, leaving me undisturbed while I worked. The only distressful thing which he was doing over months was this fugitive escape. I stayed in the first floor of my home (the ground one was rented) and a window was present in the bedroom. The cat used to sit on its pane to praise the streets and sometimes-often leaped between the grills landing straight onto the sun shed below and out of sight. This whole event used to take place within a matter of seconds and so it was very difficult to trail him where he went. His quarreling nature (recently developed) usually attracted us to the source only to find him bossing around with some other cats of the locality.

Just beside where I lived, there was this home of a very learned professor of History. My late grandmother was a good neighboring friend of this person. From a young age, as I learnt, he was a History lover and gradually become a scholar in it. He never married and always stayed single. The Professor was also a store house of international affairs as my grandmother once narrated me. I have seen him often as a kid while he used to visit our place taking an evening tea discussion with grandma. The place where he lived was equally Historical (you can compare it with a small museum!) holding a vast section of relics, artifacts, photos and whatnot. He even had some priced possessions like a letter of Napoleon Bonaparte, and a used cigar case of A.O Hume.

Everyone in the locality used to call him 'professor' although I never got a chance to know why did they call so, where and what did he teach. But that also made me start recollecting him in my writing as 'professor' – without a name. At a later age, somehow he got himself blinded and was completely out of vision in his early sixties. Professor had no family members residing at his place so there were no proper funeral procession undertaken by anyone when he died. However, his brother once came from a faraway place and shorted out the rituals to a single day, took the essentials from home and left the place as it is. The locals afterwards marked it as an abandoned area and always went past it while the stones of the place lay lifeless without their owner.

Professor never had a 'great' connection with the neighbors (except my Grandmother) as most of them avoided his intelligence, and more importantly his all-year-worn hand woven sweater and a hand-woven cap of unique structure. These attires made him distinct as anyone would tell to whom they belong. He hardly came out on streets and was mostly found either studying or rummaging through artifacts in his humble room.

To narrate in the present time, in one evening my cat made his fugitive escape (and I was sort of used to it now) through the window pane as I described earlier. I and my father were having a tea-break while the cat performed this act. Leaving the cups in half, both of us ran towards the main door and out in the streets. Father was a carrying a torch as it was darker to find a cat in the flickering street lights. We walked to check around the home for a while but there was no sign of a cat.

'The dogs are barking from there, must have seen a cat!', said father.

'Then let us check there'

'you go search towards the main streets, while I rummage through the dog-barking alley'

And as planned we parted in opposite directions. The torch was with father, so my only source of light was the street lamps. I walked attentively, slowly progressing towards the main street while a mild cat's howl caught me midway.

The sound was coming from the professor's house placed right beside where I was standing. The street lamp was atleast ten to fifteen feet away from where I was so it wasn't too much helpful for me to see a puny cat in the dark. However one thing was sure, the call was of my cat – I know his harsh and sturdy voice.

The rusty gate paving the way inside the territory of the house lay open (as it was always) and just beside the entrance there laid a small and bushy shiuli tree. I went through the dark pavement trying to place my step in the faintest of light visible. While inside the area, I squished my eyes over the walls in case it met a pair of glowing eyes of a cat.

But there was nothing to be found.

I questioned my senses to hear a howl similar to my cat and was convinced that I must have misheard something. The night wind was raging giving a hint of a rain which would visit soon. I started to retreat my steps deciding to visit my father on the other end of the street. He might have found something in relation. I was just about to pass through the rusty gate while I heard my cat's call a second time.

This time I was not mistaken. The call was pretty much clear and distinct and could be made by no other feline except mine. I re-entered the place to locate the source but something uneasy started to grip me.

The sound felt as if it was not coming from around but inside the house. 'Must have used the gaps through the collapsible gate to enter the dining space' as I thought to myself. There was a broken and netted window some few steps away from where I was standing. It directly allowed any outsider to look inside the open dining space. I decided to peep in through hoping to find a cat's figure in the dark.

There was a faint source of light coming from inside the room as if someone had lit a kerosene lamp. I smudged my glasses with my shirt's end to get a better view as I peeped further. Something really strange and as if unspeakable caught my vision. The picture within the room froze my senses and dried my throat to an indefinite extent.

Through the window and within the faint light, I found my cat sitting contently on the floor being gracefully caressed by a dark silhouette which carried a distinct look of wearing a familiar sweater and a woolen cap.

# VIII

# Room no. 207

I breached through the otter race of traffic whilst the tempered rain continued to soak both my unprotected bosom and vision. The blunt wave of noise was giving a back-up of irritation to the already existing problem. An off-road tea stall itself under the shade of un-aged banyan proved merciful to provide me a bounty. A tea would be great now, but to give the mistress of misfortune a chance to laugh at my current situation, the last two cups were served among the two men gossiping at their possible break. Unknown of their gait, I interfered on some different matter,

"Do you know any place for night stay? I'm completely soaked and won't return like this!"

One of the two answered throwing the empty paper cup on the water-clogged street, "There's the Oak's wood and Mustard N' Tarts, have you been there?"

"Nah," interrupted the other man, "Oak's wood must be closed now, and Mustard N' Tarts switched to restaurant only from the last month."

"So any other?", I was desperate.

"You would still hopefully find the Lavender's Inn open", answered the stall owner.

"Where's it?"

"Just next to your left"

I walked a few steps while covered by the banyan leftwards. Within a few yards the signboard marked the lodge's existence, "The Lavender's Inn". The rain refused to show mercy as it strengthened every moment. My staying in shade would mean diminishing my last hope of getting a bed at night. Thanking the trio in an inaudible voice amongst the traffic I splashed my way through the rain to the lodge. It was blasted with lights and ceremonial decorations and had worn the grandest of majestic galore found until here. The hallway had a small red carpet and smaller welcome mat to fulfill the continuation. The Raatrani Jasmine tied its knot with the loving rose to gratify one's senses of entering a colossal wedding. Many a cars were parked outside the appealing fortress almost blocking the entrance. This place must be witnessing a marriage tonight.

To shake hands with my thoughts of acceptance, majority of the rooms occupied were of the marriage guests, invitees and others. Although I joined in late to cherish the ceremony, the delectable aroma which struggled to prove its existence was fascinating. The tables were filled, an antonym to my stomach which demanded an appetite after the stained travel outside. Before anything, I thought it better to give my faint fortune a roll and ask for a room which I scarcely would have existed. But, this time, my fortune flickered.

"On time, just the last one left. A bit dirty, one-bedded, washroom has no geyser and..."

"I'll manage", I said interrupting the receptionist, "I just need to stay for the night."

"On your preference", and he commanded a bell boy to show me my room.

I followed his hasten steps since he didn't have to carry any luggage which I was devoid of. Every room seemed to be chaotic and laughter, mirth from every corner of the room was audible. We halted on the second floor in front of room number 206. When the bell boy started turning a key in my room's lock, I asked,

"Did the marriage take place here?"

"Yes, all the rooms occupied are by the guests only. Every arrangement were made here starting from wedding rituals to food and everything"

"Yes, it's a festive appearance therein"

He further showed the TV set, the Air Conditioner, my bed, a small wooden cupboard holding an extra pair of blanket and pillow. He asked me if I need anything else especially for dinner. I was really tired to have an arranged feast and my expenses were also pushed to wall this month, yet to be honest, I was really hungry. I ordered a full plate curry chicken and a plate of rice feeling it capable enough to satisfy my appetite. The bell boy noted it down and as per my instructions would send it to me in my room.

While he went away I took off my socks and shoes and washed my feet. I rested a bit but soon felt bored when the TV set wasn't working. I wouldn't blame the accountant as he said that this room would be devoid of certain comforts, so I decided to peep around the hallway to find something possibly interesting. I walked for a while in the multi-colored hallway decorated with various garlands. A room was particularly decorated with heavy roses, raatranis which must be for the bride-groom's rest tonight.

I met a middle aged man in a brownish suit resembling the Nazi army on a turning of the hallway. He was in high spirits – probably drunk, and was possibly some wedding guest; he started off abruptly with me,

"Enjoying the party young man?"

"I'm not into, I'm just a regular guest of the hotel.."

"Oh, if I would, I might have definitely admitted you. After a long time I think this place have witnessed such a grand celebration... Anyways, catch with you son, my wife is waiting..", and he went past. I laughed a bit at his clumsy, although well suited appearance. Perhaps, his wife would charge at him for such condition!

I retreated to my room at around nine and shortly after the door bell rang. It was the bell boy who came up with my order. I had a good dose of eating and burped over the food-laden dishes. After getting myself washed the doorbell rang once again. I opened the door to mind a middle aged women waving at me assisted by the man I already met in the hallway.

"So sorry, actually every guests were invited to the party and I didn't know anyone would have the chance to be left behind. I'm Kate and I heard from my husband Harris that you were the only guest in the whole Lavender hotel who missed the wedding."

I felt shy of such comments and a bit tinged over Mr. Harris for ear-filling this matter to his wife.

"That's none of you fault Ma'am, I signed in late for a room and thus might have missed the dine", I said.

"So that's what, you live nearby?", asked Mr. Harris

"Please, both of you do have a seat inside. Why converse like a pole", and we all had a seat in my room.

I and Mrs. Kate comforted ourselves on the couch while Mr. Harris half-laid on my bed as if his own room. I felt discontented at first but a good deal of gossip with both cheered me up. The couple was just staying next to my room and was concerned about Victor – their son's marriage. I learnt that after a wide gap they witnessed such a marriage. Within the gossip, I completely forgot about the non-functional television and malfunctioning geyser. The wedding party seemed really friendly. Our chatting was only, for once got interrupted by the bell boy who took my plates, giving me an unusual look.

The party of two left at around eleven and tight leaving me tired. The after-food-tiredness mixed with the long gossip made me highly exhausted and I fell asleep shortly afterwards.

In the morning I met with some other guests who also like the other too last night were talkative and friendly with me. There was also this bride and groom who were boarding a well-decorated car parked outside. I returned my room key to the receptionist while the bell boy stood at a distance.

"The guests seemed really contended of your services. The manager must be well managing the hotel", I remarked.

"Yes, Mr. Victor serves the people well even though he stays afar"

"What's his name again?"

"Victor Lavender, he's the current owner of the business after his parents died."

"Victor Lavender? Is his father's name Harris?"

"I wonder Sir, you know a lot, although I don't know how. Yes, you're correct Mr. Harris Lavender and Mrs. Kate Lavender were the prior owners of this hotel. It's named after them only. I personally knew Mr. Harris. After their death, the management was transferred to their only bachelor son Victor Lavender."

"But some couple came to my room last night, seemed as if from the wedding ceremony. They claimed to stay right beside my room 206, their room being 207."

"Sir, you must be mistaking something. There is no room number 207 in our hotel."

"But it can't be! What are you talking about?"

"You may check it yourself"

I briskly went upstairs leaving the bell boy behind who was also told to go with me. To both my surprise and horror, the last room I found in the entire hallway was 206. There was no such room as 207.

# IX

# Bipin Babu's Camera

Age never counts in when the subject is about 'Travel' for Bipin babu. The tour of Delhi, Bombay, Madras is completed way before at an early age, and now it was the time to travel around the locality and places in relation to it. It was decided back earlier by Bipinbabu that he would travel the faraway places while young and when old-age would strike in, the nearby places would be explored.

Bipin Chowdhury – a lone resident of the busy streets of Bagbazaar. His childless wife contracted a brain cancer five years after their marriage. She survived a few months with that ailment before her death, leaving behind Bipinbabu completely alone in the two-storey building. From that time only, travelling became Bipin babu's eternal companion.

After years he set out on a small tour for Elgin Road, the place which was about forty minutes from his residence. By travelling through two buses Bipin babu reached his destination in less than the time stipulated. He read in texts about Netaji Subhash Chandra Bose, a Great Freedom Fighter which India has witnessed. This godly personality used to stay in his residence at Elgin Road and Bipin babu had to visit this unseen place so near to his area. He travelled almost the length and breadth of the nation yet never visited this place earlier – this was a thing which even he was surprised to take account of.

Bipin babu was a true Bengali of Calcutta, and thus 'tea' was a must for him. Getting off from the transport he went on looking for a tea stall and also found one within a matter of minutes. He was devoid of any addiction while as of tea – he used to mention it as a part of culture.

Being contented by the cultural drink, Bipin babu progressed towards Netaji's place. Whatever be it, seeing through the pages of books and witnessing a thing live draws out a hell and heaven difference. The bedroom where Netaji slept, the study where he was found most of the time, the hallway passage, all seemed to have souls within them. The German car Wanderer was parked inside the compounds of Bose's residence. It was the same car which Netaji (disguised as Muhammad Ziauddin) and his nephew Sishir used to escape from English guards ordered to isolate his place. The car felt so realistic that any moment it felt as Sishir and Netaji will come out of it and move upstairs in their rooms. After spending about an hour Bipinbabu came out in the open streets. It was around eleven in the morning.

Just outside the gate of Netaji's place he witnessed a young man setting up a mix of items to make what is to be called as a (disorganized) shop. But was this shop there while Bipin babu entered Subhash's house? Maybe it was, in excitement he might have overseen it.

Pressing his back against the street wall Bipin babu met with this young man who was busy contending himself with a bidi. He was surrounded by a small heap of mixed articles, starting from household utensils, glass jars, hand woven mats, some books of unknown authors, a camera, and as such. Most of things seemed to be China made. Being some time left for lunch, Bipin babu thought it better to have a better look towards these items. After handling some of the items, the camera kept in the corner interested him. It didn't seem like an ordinary camera, maybe was some new Chinese production. Holding the camera gently in hands Bipin babu felt that while young he travelled to so many places but if at that time a camera was there, so many memories would have been picturized. It was true that he did click some pictures from other's camera, but today those photos are nowhere to be found. What would be the fault if he had one while travelling earlier? He thought to buy the device, but at a second instance thought that his travelling had almost seized by now and hence the camera would feel the dust in his home if bought. However, again he thought that atleast the tours of Calcutta would be captured if he had one camera.

Having little or no knowledge about a camera, he started at the shopkeeper with some weird questions,

'That's a camera right? So, it clicks pictures, isn't it?'

Throwing the bidi from his mouth in an untidy place nearby the shop-man answered,

'It's a Polaroid Camera, a Japanese device. That's the last piece left'

Naturally he didn't understand a specialty which the shop-man might be describing about the camera so he asked again,

'What is meant by Polaroid?'

'The photo clicked through this camera directly comes out in hand within a matter of seconds'

'What! Within a matter of seconds?', said an excited Bipin babu.

The shop-keeper took the camera off Bipin babu's grip, dusted it for a while and then asked him stand in front of the news bulletin board which was directly facing the shop. Bipin babu did so while the shop-man clicked a photo. A flick was heard, and there came out a black square-shaped paper in his hand. Within a few seconds, the blackish tone faded to reveal a clear photo of Bipin Babu in the paper.

Bipin babu didn't conversed further. Without a bargain he bought the item at a comparative higher price than expected. He somehow figured that the camera was not something to be bargained of. Landing off at Bagbaazar, Bipin babu started searching something worthy enough to

take photo of. After buying a new item Bipin babu was eager to show it to someone, but he lived too much in solitude within his society to do that. Finding nothing worthy enough to take photo of, he drifted towards his home alley and found a black cat sleeping on a low wall. Being sympathetic, firstly he thought not to bother the cat, but then thought it was deep in sleep so a click was less likely to disturb it.

The camera shutter flicked. Bipin babu waited for the paper to come out of the camera like a thirsty man in desert waiting for a drop of water. Receiving the sheet in hand he walked off towards his home. The photo would also come in it till then.

The first thing he did after opening his entrance door was look in the picture. But what is this? Where is the cat? There was only a wall and the visible garden behind it. Did the animal switched position while the photo was clicked? Must be it, but even without that cat, the simple picture taken of the wall and the garden behind seemed so mesmerizing. By clicking such a lovely photo, Bipinbabu's confidence increased. He became as much excited as a child gets after receiving the toy he wants. Starting from his rooms, to doors, to windows, almirah, study table, even the doormat didn't escape from his camera's lens.

Hovering around the house with the camera, he overlooked the time. He started with the lunch past four – he never remembers to be this late before. The interest in food today seemed no match in front of clicking photos from that camera. Whatever be the schedule of everything, it was customary for Bipin Babu to sit on his couch at five in the evening, his hand occupied by a cup of tea. Having two-three sips, he started to look at his clicked photos. Every photo tempted him to take more, the door, the mat, the windows, the almirah, everything was so well captured. However, the photo of the study room disturbed him a bit.

The picture witnessed a messy study table with few books kept dismantled over it. The pen-pencils were not in their usual places, an old register and a travel book was seen lying open. When did all these happen? As far remembered he never used his study table throughout the day. Was the table still in such condition now? Inquired by this thought, he visited his study room only to get amazed that everything there was neat and clean. Strangely enough no books were scattered and nothing was untidy. So was untidy when he was busy clicking the photos and later he arranged the table? With advancing age, Bipin Babu as if was losing his memory faster than expected. He turned down the matter marking it as a product of his unnatural forgetfulness. Moreover, the amount of play he did with just a camera made him realize his childish acts.

Having the tea finished, he went out for a walk in his locality – however, didn't forget to take the camera with him. What if something photo-worthy comes in sight? On the other half of the day, the place where that Black cat was sleeping now had a red car parked in front of the alley opening. Did his neighbor Shyam Babu buy a new car? Whatever be the case, the red color was very tempting; just like the reddish die present in the feet of a new-bride.

So what else is need to spoken of? When Almirah, doormat, window, study table became objects of photo, then why not a brand new car? The camera flicker was heard. Just like before, Bipin Babu waited for the sheet to come out of the device. It came out within seconds and he waited further for the picture of the car to appear in it. But what is it? Almost half-a-minute passed but there was no sign of an image in the black paper. This was a thing Bipin Babu was noticing earlier. After each and every shot, the photograph was taking an increasing time to appear in-place of the black space. After spending five more minutes in various thoughts, Bipin Babu wandered whether the camera had broken or something. Well even if it was out-of-service, it wasn't too much unusual as he was using the Japanese device throughout the day without rest. Was it for this reason that he camera was malfunctioning? Or something else? Bipin Babu couldn't figure out.

He briskly went inside his room. The price of the camera was too much to malfunction so early, and as so, he decided that he would visit the seller at Elgin road the very next day. Suddenly Bipin Babu was reminded of his stock-pile of books which he bought while travelling in his youth. What if any of them had a remedy for this malfunctioning device? Then he wouldn't have to take the hassle to visit the shop-keeper at Elgin Road again.

Even after spending a few hours, he failed to find a suitable book which would mend this problem. He also looked down his table for a separate rack of books, but instead found there an old register. After rummaging through it for a while, he left it open on his table. Interestingly he found an unread travel book in his pile and got himself contented in it for a while.

It was about nine at night. After so much of strain today, the body wouldn't take more. There was no energy left for him to re-arrange his books so he went to dinner. A bowl of Dahl, some Spinach and a couple of potato strip fries made up his dinner. Bipin Babu closed to his bedroom bringing in a glass of water with him. He kept it on the bed-side table. All the photos clicked today were paper-weighed on that table.

After preparing the bed, he sat upright on it drinking from the glass of water and looking through the photos all over again. The picture of the study table clicked earlier seemed as if he witnessed the scene just now, that open register, the travel guide,.. but he was dumbstruck when his eyes met with the last photo clicked today. This was the photo of that new-red car clicked in the evening. However, it didn't look new in the photo now.

The photo showed a medium-size crack in the frontal glass, a wiper was also looking bent. But the thing which was even more terrifying was another coat of red over the red vehicle, and was definitely blood. Although to a smaller extent, this was perceived as such.

The glass stood frozen in his hands. Bipin Babu's face also turned pale. The touch of terror was clearly visible in his portrait. Being too much terrified, he flung the photo across the room. Somehow, finishing the remaining water in glass, he hung his legs from the bed's end, his sweaty face staring blankly at the floor. The bed-light was still turned on.

Indeed, who would sleep comfortably after witnessing such an unusual image? Stomping the remaining photos off the bed to the table beside him he switched off the bed-light with much difficulty. After changing sides in the bed for about half-an-hour, he unknowingly went off to sleep.

As per habit, he woke up half-past-seven in the morning. It is said, with light comes courage – same was the case with Bipin Babu. Trying not to think much of the last night's incident, he grabbed the photos from his table and set out for Elgin Road. He must get hold of that camera-seller; god knows what kind of thing he sold to him!

He went out without having anything in the morning. Through the same two-bus journey he reached Elgin Road and shortly went to search for the news-bulletin board. He knew that the seller was sitting near to it yesterday. But today, that small shop was nowhere to be found. He must have thought of it in the first place. The seller must be a cheater who sold him such a defective device for such a high price! Even if the device in its malfunctioning state worked for days, some of the problems would have been compensated.

He asked the owner of the tea stall, the place from where he consumed tea the last day,

'Yesterday there was a young man selling a variety of mixed Chinese item next to the wall of Netaji's residence. You know where he is now?'

'The place where you are stating is forbidden for business. If that was so, I myself would have shifted my shop next to Netaji's wall – the sales would increase'

'What are you talking about? He was sitting yesterday just next to that news-bulletin board!'

'I'm sorry Sir; really I've seen no one'

Bipin Babu was not at all satisfied. He went on asking a few more stalls in line but no answer satisfied him. The shop owner claimed that they had seen no one like that.

In the busy streets of Calcutta, who is the one who keeps record of small business firms and where, when are they established? It was probably one of the reasons why Bipin Babu was unable to find that unidentified seller. The most unworthy part which he was feeling now that even after coming so long with such anxiety, he'll have to return home empty handed.

After boarding the bus for going back home, a strange mystery begun to turn within Bipin Babu. The camera was not capturing the photo as it as but is printing out something different. Some things were the same, while some were different. He recalled the incident of his study table from yesterday. The table was neatly arranged, yet the picture came out showing it all messed up. He pulled out that image from his pocket and felt that this same scene he had witnessed – yes exactly! His table was exactly this kind of untidy when in the evening he was searching for a book that would mend his camera! The photo felt as if it was forecasting an event which is to come. After boarding off from the bus, he recalled another incident of that black cat sitting on the wall of his alley yesterday. The picture clicked had no cat in it, but it was always sitting on that wall. Really strange, did the image intend a future event of the cat when it will disappear from that wall to some other place?

Completely entangled within thoughts, he turned towards his alley turning the camera abruptly in his hands. Just after the turn, he was being hit by a speeding car coming from the opposite direction. The camera flew off from his hands and hit on the car's frontal glass pane. The driver and few more neighbors clumped around the spot.

During his last seconds, Bipin Babu noticed something. This car from yesterday had a wiper broken and had conceived a medium-sized crack on the front window.

This picture was already familiar to him.

# X

# A Research on God's death

I was in my mid twenties when Professor Beck came to visit India. He was in charge of the Department of Ancient Studies in a German governmental research center. His real name was Professor Schmidt Hoffman Becker. I was under his guidance while in Germany completing my Masters in Historical Researches.

I received a letter from him a month ago where he wrote that he would visit Gujarat shortly for some of his research. He would be accompanied by two of his men. If I want, I would visit him on the specified date in the afternoon at Surat. While working with him, I knew Professor to be a skeptical sort of person, up for collecting that information which was not found in History texts. He had his philosophy that what has already been found is written, and what is to yet be found, is waiting to be written. I have went through his researches in various German territories, world war afflicted areas, the worshipping of black holes (he believes there are countless black holes), facts or lies regarding the lost city of Atlantis, the hidden priceless articles in Budapest, and even various theories regarding world leaders. He wrote on various researches about Hitler. One of them said, Hitler once tried to teach animals how to read thus would work as handy spies in war times. He also stated that the United States once tried to feminize Hitler by using some specially prepared laboratory drugs.

He used to ask me very little about India when I was there in German, a fact which was contradictory to most German students there who often used to ask me about India and its rich culture, History. Professor, as I reckoned, kept a stash of those information which the world was yet to know.

When I met him at Surat, he was assisted by his two men Adolf and Kaiser (Interestingly both the names are of the diplomats who once ruled the German Empire!). I grabbed his hand, greeting him being as a loyal student. It wasn't until in a room of Surat when I found the reason why Professor was here. Adolf and Kaiser were outside somewhere and we both were sitting on two oppositely facing couch, accompanied by a relishing tea of Gujarat in hand.

'This time it will be remarkable, I disbelief what general mass thinks of this. I know what I know', started Professor Beck, holding the tea cup in a slanted manner, his mood visibly travelling elsewhere.

'Up for something new Professor? Or it's just a break this time?'

'Those two supports, cost me a real fortune. All expenses of them down from Berlin to Gujarat were on me, do you still have any reasons to believe that I came here just for a trip?'

Professor was always that much crooked. Infact, I would say, he straightened a bit, as he was even more crooked while I was studying under him.

'I didn't know you paid their travel Professor. I'm sorry.'

'You must be. Keep these matters of so less an importance aside and focus on what was told, way, way much earlier...'

He meant History, as always. He used this same style when I was under him learning various matters. I was tempted to ask the reason of his visit to India, but before my interrogation he answered himself.

'I came here for something which killed Krishna'

'Krishna?'

'Get out of my room if you don't know Krishna!'

'I never said so, I was just curious about which Krishna you meant.'

'How many Krishna you know in your History?'

'If you mean the God Krishna, yes I know that mythological figure.'

Professor Beck banged his half-empty cup in such a way which scared me a bit. His fury was further visible in the later statements,

'I knew that all my efforts to make you understand History has lost its value. You're still a modern lad, History is not a subject for you.. Go study stupid fairy tales and mix them up with real historical records.

What makes you think that Krishna was a mythological figure? Even Cindrella, Tinker Bell, and that stupid beast and that girl from the tale 'Beauty and the Beast' are folks, why aren't they worshipped? Even they are praised by most lads as godly then why so they aren't worshipped? You are unworthy to call yourself an Indian'

I had no answers, so kept listening to whatever he said.

'Just from His appearance in Indian History Mahabharata, Lord Vishnu's eighth incarnation was originally born on earth. Krishna appeared in the city of Mathura, present day Uttar Pradesh. He was from the Yadu clan, the dynasty of Ugrasena – being His maternal-grandfather, and Vasudeva His father', he finished the tea and continued, 'After years of His childhood days, He appeared on the side of Pandavas in the Great Battle of Kurukshetra. He was the reason why the small force of Pandavas was able to defeat the opposing Kaurava forces with outnumbered military and expert generals'.

I never ever thought that Professor would drag his research work over some Indian Gods. Even if I keep aside that fact, the Historical records which he kept on broadcasting had something which glued my interest.

'When the 100 Kaurava sons' army were defeated by mere 5 Panadavas' army – they were brothers, Gandhari – the mother of the Kaurava came to the battlefield. When she found that all her sons were dead, she cursed Krishna that 36 years from now on He will meet death and all His Yadava clan would be destroyed therein.'

'And then?'

'Then what? Krishna even though the Supreme Lord of Universes, accepted the curse as He claims death to be inevitable. He also reckoned that the Yadu clan was getting powerful under His supervision, and before this group could cause tantrum over other sects, He must disappear from this material world and the Yadus could met their inevitable fate'

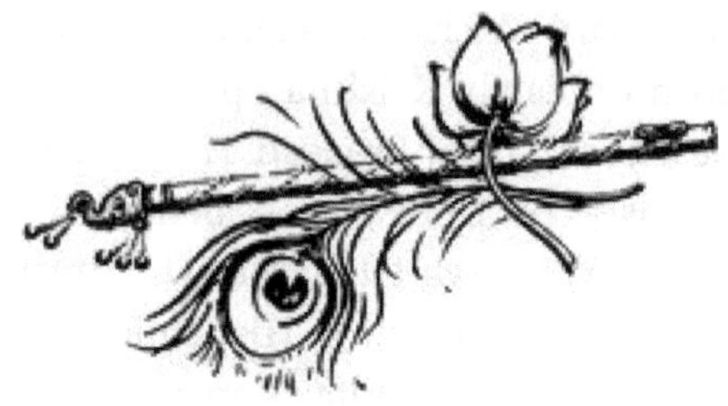

'Did the curse worked?'

'Curses have scientific explanations. When one acts as per prescribed laws, he/she invokes the cyclic movement of the all-time rotational *Kal Chakra*, or the wheel of time. Newton stated this functioning of this Chakra to an infinitely smaller extent through his third-law which states that 'Every action has an equal and opposite reaction'. The living matter and it's functioning is non-different from science and thus this law works too well in materialistic lives. The curse inflicted standing on truth by Gandhari invoked the *Kal Chakra* and thus Krishna was just told the reason of how He could meet the inevitable death. Nothing unnatural in it, so it works that way.'

'After that?'

'After Krishna left for His kingdom in Dwarka, one of His sons played a trick amongst the group of most divine Indian Sages. Among a group, one son of Krishna pretended to act like a pregnant women and presented himself foolishly before one of the Great Sage. The Sage through his divine abilities was able to conjure the trick being played and thus he cursed that acting boy to give birth to a block of material which would be the reason for the destruction of the Yadu Dynasty. The boys thought it as a joke but the boy who pretended to be the women went through actual labor and produced a lump of mysterious metal. Terrified by the fact that this metal could lead the end of the Yadu clan, the boys broke the block into fine pieces and flowed them in the river.'

He continued after a short gap, 'While most of the pieces were washed in the water, a short piece among the granules made its way into the mouth of a fish. This fish was later caught by a hunter named Jara who split opened its belly to find this metal. He prepared the metal by mending it as the tip of his arrow, thus creating a deadly and poisonous weapon which would be used for hunting.'

I was getting gradually amazed. Even I was unaware of such a History, being an Indian myself. I think Professor Beck was true; I still had lot to learn. I was instinctive of what would have happened next so I started at him and this act, I think, provoked his interest to tell me more,

'Meanwhile the Yadu members were on a vacation near a water side. A small quarrel rose among who fought truthfully on behalf of the Pandavas. This small issue turned into a bigger tide when one fought with each other proving who fought more righteously. As they were on their so called holiday, they were devoid of weapons. So they uprooted small canes, tree barks and stoke each other. Within some time, all of them killed each other leaving two members who went onto Krishna to inform what had happened to the Yadu clan. So theorists say that the Yadu people drank the water beside which they were present. This water had that strange metal dust mixed within it, earlier being drowned by Krishna's kids. This certain element might have caused senselessness or a sort of grave intoxication which resulted in such a massacre.'

'So what happened to Krishna then?'

'Krishna as I said was informed of His clan's deathly condition by the survivors of the fight. He smiled knowing what was to come and went off to the forest to perform meditation. When He sat meditating, His all-attracting left foot swayed among the bushes. Jara, the hunter through a distance thought it to be some priceless deer's ear, and thus he shot the arrow made of that mystic metal towards Krishna's direction. The arrow went deep into Krishna's left foot from where a stream of blood flowed. Jara ran to the spot only to see the gravest of act which he had done. He begged in front of Krishna to forgive him, whilst Krishna forgiving him said that it was all known to Him. Krishna said that Jara was Bali in his previous birth and was killed by His previous incarnation Ram Chandra's arrow from behind. This was just a Karmic, that is, reactionary act which followed this time. This is how Krishna left the mortal body in earth.'

'Most amazing information which I ever received till yet! Thank you so much Professor Beck for telling me all this. But I still have something to ask you, may I?'

'Yes, of course'

'What are you after, I mean, through this History what are you trying to decipher or research upon?'

'That I've already told you'

'If you may, I mean, tell me once more...'

'Didn't I say that I'm after something which killed Krishna?'

'You mean...'

'Yes', he stood up from his seat and continued, 'Jara's arrowhead. That mysterious material. I'm after that. This is something which most Historians omits or doesn't consider being something worth of so much an importance. That metal, non-metal or whatever mysterious element which it is created of, has some divine abilities. I'm too old now to explore like earlier so brought those too men. They were way to excited about my research and I'm hence afraid of what they might do without my permission'

'But Professor, what made you think something like that has still managed to exist?'

'The same spirit which made Hitler carry out his secret expedition in the city of Sambhala, Uttar Pradesh. He was onto something which is forecasted. As per scriptures, Lord Vishnu's 10th incarnation – Lord Kalki is to appear in the city Sambhala.'

I was perplexed. Not because of what Professor was saying, but because of perceiving the fact that how much void my knowledge was. After about few hours of discussing with Professor, I asked about Kaiser and Adolf. They were supposed to visit us by the evening. We had our meal while a notice came from a local informant who told that two men were found dead near the Bholka Tirtha, an area near the western banks of Gujurat. It was about 4 Kilometers from the famous Somnath Temple of India.

'Would be none other than Kaiser, and Adolf. Of course...', stated Professor, 'I warned them not to. Bholka Tirtha is the same place where Sri Krishna's mortal body was being hit by Jara's arrow. One trying to interfere in the scene without proper knowledge would meet the same fate.'

The morning news cleared my doughts and proved what Professor said. Indeed they were Adolf and Kaiser who were allegedly killed by something mysterious which struck on their left legs. No weapon, nothing was found sticking but the post-mortem says the damaged area of the foots had a distinct mark of getting struck with something like a sharp arrow.

9 798887 726960

Printed by Libri Plureos GmbH in Hamburg,
Germany